This toddler talkabout
belongs to

Gareth

D0031836

Using this book

Ladybird's toddler talkabouts are ideal for encouraging children to talk about what they see. Bold, colourful pictures and simple questions help to develop early learning skills – such as matching, counting and detailed observation.

Look at this book together. First talk about the pictures yourself, and point out things to look at. Let your child take her* time. With encouragement, she will start to join in, talking about the familiar things in the pictures. Help her to count objects, to look for things that match, and to talk about what is going on in the picture stories.

To avoid the clumsy use of he/she, the child is referred to as 'she'.
Toddler talkabouts are suitable for both boys and girls.

Publishers note:
The animals included in this book do not originate from the same habitat but have been included because they are recognised favourites with young children.

Acknowledgement: Cover illustration by Terry Burton

Published by Ladybird Books Ltd
27 Wrights Lane London W8 5TZ
A Penguin Company
3 5 7 9 10 8 6 4 2
© LADYBIRD BOOKS LTD MCMXCVIII

Printed in Italy

I like
wild
animals

illustrated by Richard Morgan
and Andy Everitt-Stewart

Ladybird

Who can you see
in the jungle?

How many animals can you count?

1 one

2 two

3
three

4
four

5
five

How many legs does the zebra have?

How many teeth does the hippo have?

What's happening here? Tell the story.

What colour is the frog?

What other colours can you see?

Find another...

zebra

lion

parrot

How many tigers are there in the box?

How many now?

Poor Lion! Tell the story.

What baby animals can you see?

Who has furry skin and who has smooth skin?

Who's hiding in the jungle?